DREAMWORKS PICTURES and NICKELODEON MOVIES
PRESENT

Hotel For Dogs™

THE MOVIE STORYBOOK

Adapted by Tracey West
Based on the book by Lois Duncan
Screenplay by Jeff Lowell and Bob Schooley & Mark McCorkle

Simon Spotlight
New York   London   Toronto   Sydney

Based on the movie *Hotel For Dogs*™

SIMON SPOTLIGHT
An imprint of Simon & Schuster Children's Publishing Division
1230 Avenue of the Americas, New York, New York 10020
TM Paramount Pictures. © 2008 DreamWorks LLC. All Rights Reserved.
All rights reserved, including the right of reproduction in whole or in part in any form.
SIMON SPOTLIGHT and colophon are registered trademarks of Simon & Schuster, Inc.
Manufactured in the United States of America
First Edition 10 9 8 7 6 5 4 3 2 1
ISBN-13: 978-1-4169-7513-7
ISBN-10: 1-4169-7513-6

No matter what life threw at them, sixteen-year-old Andi, her younger brother, Bruce, and their dog, Friday, always stuck together. They were a family, and Andi was determined to keep it that way.

After losing their parents years ago, Andi vowed to do what-
ever it took to protect her younger brother. Over the years
they'd had lots of foster parents, but nobody ever wanted to
adopt them. Of course, Andi made their social worker, Bernie,
promise to find them a home together.

Until then Andi and Bruce had to stick it out with the Scudders, their newest set of foster parents. Lois and Carl Scudder cared about their band more than they cared about anything—including Andi and Bruce.

It was getting more and more difficult for Bernie to place them in foster homes together. He warned them that until he could find them the perfect parents, they needed to stick it out with Lois and Carl; otherwise they'd be split up.

The Scudders didn't like dogs, either. So Andi and Bruce had to keep Friday a secret, hiding him in the alley behind the apartment building.

Friday was good at hiding—except when there was food around! One morning Bruce woke up to the smell of breakfast and no Friday. Bruce headed into the kitchen, knowing that Friday had followed the scent there.

"Friday!" Bruce cried out when he saw the pup, thankful that Lois hadn't noticed him yet.

"What?" Lois asked, turning to face Bruce.

"I said, 'What's the day after Thursday?'" Andi asked as she joined the diversion away from the dog.

"Friday!" Bruce answered, smiling.

"Thank you!" yelled Andi, trying to keep Lois from noticing Friday.

"What's the matter with you two?" Lois barked. Behind her, Friday had climbed onto the stove and was busy gobbling up her bacon.

"We're just excited to be here!" Bruce chimed in.

"That reminds me of a funny story," Andi began, attempting to keep Lois's attention away from Bruce while he quickly scooped up Friday and put him back on the window ledge.

Thankfully Lois didn't see Friday—but it was a close call.

Still hungry, Friday took off in search of more food. He hurried down the streets, sniffing until he ran into Max, the not-so-friendly animal control officer!

"You make it too easy," said Max. He grabbed Friday and hauled him off to the pound.

CENTRAL CITY ANIMAL CONTROL

Andi and Bruce looked everywhere for Friday. They asked Mark, the guy working at the grocery store nearby, if he'd seen Friday, but he hadn't. Next they stopped in the pet store to put up some flyers.

"We're looking for our dog," Andi told Dave, one of the guys working there. "I don't suppose you've seen him?" she continued, handing Dave a flyer.

"Friday. Really? Where'd that name come from?" he asked.

"It's a long story," Andi replied. "We should get going."

"Good luck finding him," Dave said with a smile.

Finally Andi and Bruce made their way to the pound, just in time to see Max putting Friday into a cage!

"Just bring your parents in and you can have your dog back," said Jake, the man behind the desk.

Andi had to think fast. "I'm going to level with you," she told Jake. "That dog means everything to us. My parents aren't coming. If I told you the real reason why, you'd start crying, I'd start crying, and it would be a big, miserable mess. So I'm going to give you every penny I have in the world, and you're going to find it in your heart to let that dog out."

Jake gave Friday to Andi and Bruce.
But they still had a problem. Where were they going to keep him? They couldn't take him home, and they couldn't let him hide out in the alley anymore—it was too risky!

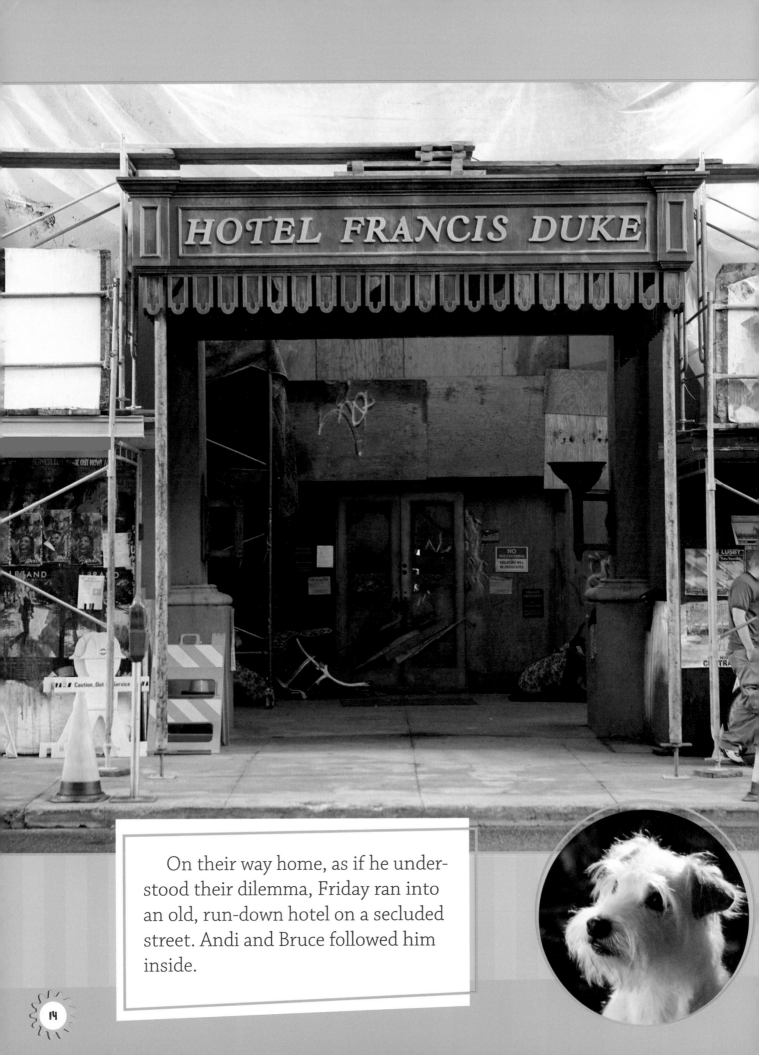

On their way home, as if he understood their dilemma, Friday ran into an old, run-down hotel on a secluded street. Andi and Bruce followed him inside.

Bruce turned on his flashlight. A noise floated down the stairs.

"Did you hear that?" Bruce asked.

The sound of footsteps came closer and closer. A creature came out of the shadows. Bruce shone his flashlight on it, his heart pounding.

It was a tiny Boston terrier! Behind her came a big black mastiff. Then Friday burst out of the darkness. He ran up to the two dogs. They all sniffed each other, tails wagging.

"What about leaving Friday here tonight?" Bruce suggested.

The next morning Andi and Bruce went back to the hotel. They brought some leftovers from Lois's inedible dinner to feed the dogs. Bruce placed the food in front of the dogs. Nothing happened.

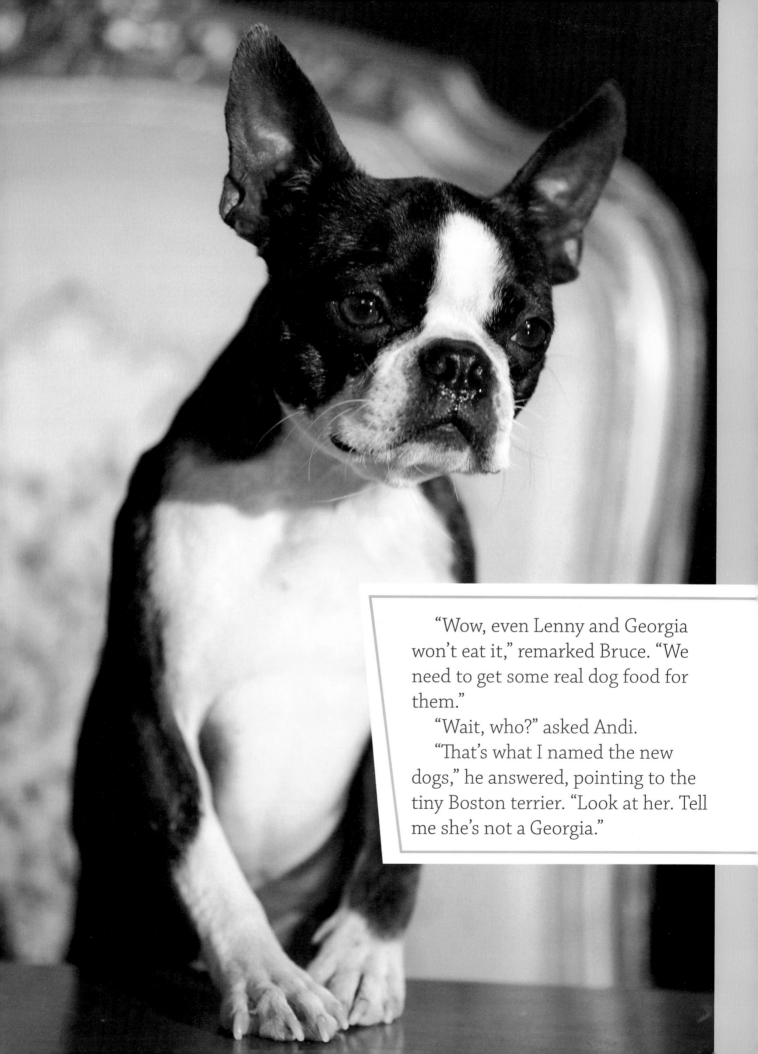

"Wow, even Lenny and Georgia won't eat it," remarked Bruce. "We need to get some real dog food for them."

"Wait, who?" asked Andi.

"That's what I named the new dogs," he answered, pointing to the tiny Boston terrier. "Look at her. Tell me she's not a Georgia."

Andi went back to the neighborhood pet store to get some real dog food, and she saw Dave again.

"Why do you need eighty pounds of dog food?" he asked her.

"My parents love animals," Andi lied. "We have this big yard, so we just rescue dogs all the time."

"All the time? You know what? Come with me," Dave said.

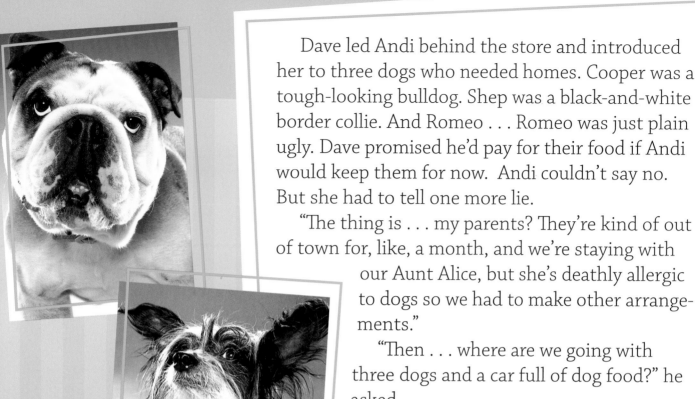

Dave led Andi behind the store and introduced her to three dogs who needed homes. Cooper was a tough-looking bulldog. Shep was a black-and-white border collie. And Romeo . . . Romeo was just plain ugly. Dave promised he'd pay for their food if Andi would keep them for now. Andi couldn't say no. But she had to tell one more lie.

"The thing is . . . my parents? They're kind of out of town for, like, a month, and we're staying with our Aunt Alice, but she's deathly allergic to dogs so we had to make other arrangements."

"Then . . . where are we going with three dogs and a car full of dog food?" he asked.

So they loaded up Dave's truck and headed to the hotel. Little did they know that Dave's coworker Heather was following them.

Luckily she promised to help keep their secret.

Now Andi and Bruce had a big family of dogs to take care of. Walking and feeding all the new dogs was a lot of work. The alarm clock woke them up at five every morning.

"We can't do this five times a day," Andi complained as they walked the dogs down the street.

Bruce knew Andi was right. Fortunately Bruce was a bit of an inventor, so he got busy in his workshop at the hotel. He knew he could make some ordinary household objects perform a few tricks that would make their lives a whole lot easier.

A few days later the alarm clock rang—in the dog hotel! Bruce's feeding machine sprung into action. Cans of food spun around on a wheel and dumped food into each dog dish.

Andi and Bruce didn't have to wake up early. The machine did all the work for them!

Then Bruce trained the dogs to use his next invention—the Poop Room. The dogs did their business in designated spots. A conveyor belt took the waste to a hairdryer that sealed it in shrink wrap. No smell, no mess!

Bruce also invented an automatic fetching machine that threw newspapers for the dogs to catch. He even made some fake sheep for Shep so she could practice herding!

Thanks to Bruce, the dogs were happy. Andi and Bruce were happy too. Heather and Dave were there to help with all of the dogs. Even Mark from the corner deli came by and offered a hand. Together they felt like one big family.

Every day their family got bigger. Every time the kids came across a stray dog that needed a home, they brought it back to the hotel. Soon the hotel was full!

One day Andi and Bruce's social worker, Bernie, came to the Scudders' apartment.

"I found the perfect foster parents for you!" he told them.

Andi and Bruce were so excited—they couldn't wait to leave the Scudders.

"And I'll still be able to see you guys now and then because your new place is only three hours away," Bernie told them excitedly.

Suddenly this didn't seem like such a good plan after all. Three hours away? Andi and Bruce wanted a new family, but they couldn't leave the dogs.

"I don't know," Bruce told Bernie. "We like the area."

"Carl's and Lois's singing really grows on you," Andi said. "I'm afraid we're going to have to pass."

Bernie couldn't believe what he was hearing. From the moment he placed Andi and Bruce with the Scudders, the kids had been begging to get out.

"This opportunity is not going to last, and if things don't work out here, you've probably blown your final shot to stay together," he warned them. "I just hope you know what you're doing."

The door slammed behind Bernie as he left the siblings wondering if they'd really done the right thing.

Andi smiled at Bruce and assured him, "We're going to be fine."

But Andi wasn't sure if she had made the right decision at all. She was just putting on a brave face for Bruce. Later on, back at the hotel, she sat on the roof with Friday, thinking about the future. Then Dave came up and sat down next to her.

"Are you ever going to tell me why you named him Friday?" he asked.

"Someday," Andi answered. She didn't want Dave to know the truth about her life—not yet. She had managed to keep everything a secret so far. . . .

"So hey, listen, are you doing anything tomorrow night?" he asked her. "A friend of mine's having a party."

Andi smiled. "Just tell me where it is, and I'll meet you there."

The next night Andi put on a beautiful old dress she found upstairs in one of the hotel rooms.

At the party Dave introduced her to everyone. She was having a great time, even developing a bit of a crush on Dave.

Then suddenly, something awful happened. She'd been spotted. A boy, Jason, started walking toward them . . . and he knew her secret.

"You live in my grandmother's building with the Scudders, right?" he asked.

"No, I'm over on Oak. But I have one of those faces," Andi lied.

"No, you live with the Scudders," Jason insisted. "They're your foster parents."

Andi tried to cover up the truth with more lies, but it was too late. Her secret was out, and she was thoroughly embarrassed. She turned to grab a drink, trying to leave the conversation gracefully, but she was too nervous. She accidentally bumped into the drink tray, sending glasses flying and covering her beautiful dress in punch. She ran out of the party in tears.

Back at the Scudders' apartment, Bruce was experiencing some difficulties too. Lois caught him taking an old hair dryer from the house—which he intended to use for one of his inventions.

"Why are you stealing my hair dryer?" Lois asked.

"It's an old one you don't even use," Bruce pointed out.

But Lois was furious. "I open my heart to you, and you steal from me! I'm calling Bernie. I want you both out of my house!"

Instead of waiting around to get thrown out, Bruce ran out of the apart-ment and headed toward the hotel. He didn't know it, but Lois and Carl were following him. When they finally wound up at their destination, they were shocked at what they saw.

"I can't believe they own a hotel!" Carl exclaimed.

"Carl, you're an idiot," Lois answered, annoyed.

The dogs at the hotel were out of control! A group of dogs had spilled a bag of food all over the floor. Georgia and a big dog named Henry were fighting over a bone. The dogs were chasing each other, crashing into Bruce's inventions, and knocking over cans of paint that the kids were using to repaint the walls.

Bruce frantically tried to calm down the dogs, but was having no success. Then, luckily, Andi showed up, having returned from the party early.

"What happened?" she asked.

"Don't ask," Bruce replied. "What happened to you?"

"Don't ask," she answered.

All of a sudden they heard the scream of sirens outside. Two police cars pulled up. Andi and Bruce knew they were in trouble. Their big secret wasn't a secret anymore.

The police took them down to the station, and soon Bernie showed up.

"Are you going to send us to that nice other house now?" Bruce asked hopefully.

But it was too late for that. The Scudders refused to take the kids back even for a few nights, despite how hard Bernie pleaded with them.

"I'm sorry. There's nothing left I can do," Bernie said sadly.

There was no place for Andi and Bruce to go together. They would have to split up.

Andi hugged her brother.

"I let you down," she said. "I was supposed to keep us together and protect us."

"We had to protect the dogs," Bruce said. "We did exactly what we were supposed to do. If we had it to do over again, I'd do the same thing."

Animal control took all of the dogs out of the hotel and put them in cages in the pound—including Friday, who was doing his best to eavesdrop on the humans' conversation.

"Tomorrow morning is the last day for all of them," one of the guys said.

Tomorrow? In a flash Friday slipped out of his leash and snuck out through the employee entrance. He had to find Andi and Bruce!

Friday ran through the streets of the town. He couldn't find Andi and Bruce anywhere. But he did find someone he knew: Dave.

Dave and Friday tracked down Andi in her new foster home.

"How'd you get him out?" Andi asked.

"He got himself out," Dave said. "Found me. We went for a drive. Found you."

"At this point I think both of you might be better off without me," Andi said. Then she softened. "You wanted to know why we named him Friday? My real parents used to take me and Bruce out for a picnic every Friday night. One week we're at a lake, and this little stray gets into our food. Tiny little puppy ate four people's food. The thing wanted to run away, but it was too full. What could we do? We had to adopt it. Our mom came up with the perfect name—Friday."

Andi patted Friday on the head. Friday barked, and they headed out to rescue the dogs.

First, they got Bruce out of his new foster home. Dave drove his Dogmobile. They picked up Mark and Heather and pulled up in front of the dog pound. They didn't have a real plan yet, but they had to get those dogs out of there!

"I got sausage!" Mark announced, holding up a sack.

But Heather had an even better idea. She knocked on the window of the pound. "Fire!" she yelled.

The guy in the office panicked and ran out of the building. Finally the coast was clear.

Andi and the others ran into the pound and freed the dogs. Bruce dangled the sausage out of the back of the van. The dogs ran after them down the street. They were running, all right, but not toward the sausages. In fact, they didn't seem to care about food at all. . . .

"Home! They're going home," Bruce said. The dogs were running toward the hotel!

The dogs scrambled into the hotel. Andi, Bruce, and their friends followed them. So did the animal control officers—and the police!

"We'll have these dangerous canines rounded up in no time," the officer promised the crowd that had formed outside.

"No! Wait!" Bruce and Andi yelled.

Just then one of the animal control guys grabbed Friday. Andi tried to stop him, but was caught by a police officer. Everyone tried to tell their side of the story to the police as a crowd gathered outside the hotel. Suddenly, there was a shout from the top of the stairs.

"Stop!"

It was Bernie!

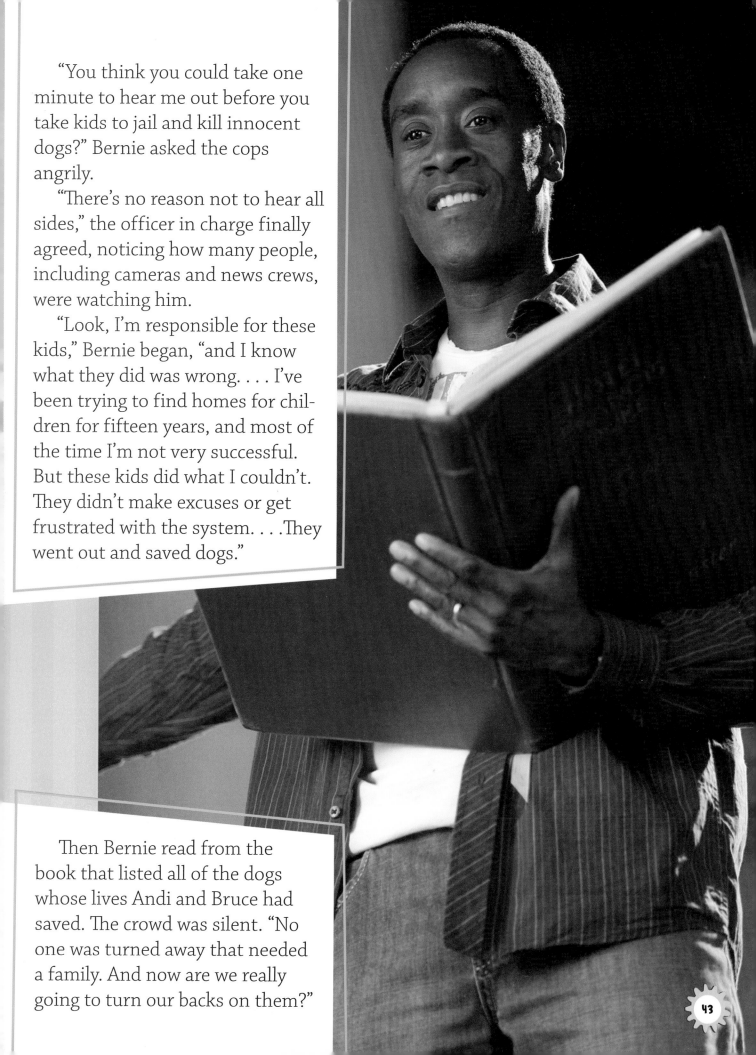

"You think you could take one minute to hear me out before you take kids to jail and kill innocent dogs?" Bernie asked the cops angrily.

"There's no reason not to hear all sides," the officer in charge finally agreed, noticing how many people, including cameras and news crews, were watching him.

"Look, I'm responsible for these kids," Bernie began, "and I know what they did was wrong. . . . I've been trying to find homes for children for fifteen years, and most of the time I'm not very successful. But these kids did what I couldn't. They didn't make excuses or get frustrated with the system. . . .They went out and saved dogs."

Then Bernie read from the book that listed all of the dogs whose lives Andi and Bruce had saved. The crowd was silent. "No one was turned away that needed a family. And now are we really going to turn our backs on them?"

Within seconds the crowd was marching into the hotel to scope out the home that Andi and Bruce had created, marveling at all of Bruce's inventions, and giving the dogs a little tender loving care.

The story of the dog hotel made the news. People all over town were rooting for Andi, Bruce, and the dogs.

Andi and Bruce were happy for the dogs, even though they knew they would have to go back to their separate foster homes.

Then Bernie gave them some good news. Really good news.

"I found you some real parents," Bernie told them. He and his wife had decided to adopt Andi and Bruce!

Soon the Hotel For Dogs held a grand re-opening. The old, run-down hotel was now clean and beautiful. The dogs there had a safe, happy place to live until they were adopted.

Some of the dogs got to help out too. Georgia made a great bellhop!

The dogs finally had a chance to find a new family. And for the first time in a long time, Andi and Bruce felt like they were in a real family too.

They still had Friday. But now they had brand-new parents who really cared about them. They had great friends in Heather, Mark, and Dave. And they had a hotel full of dogs!